Rabén & Sjögren Bokförlag
Box 2052, 103 12 Stockholm
rabensjogren.se

*Rabén & Sjögren Bokförlag is part of*
*Norstedts Förlagsgrupp AB, founded in 1823*

# Pippi

## goes shopping

# ASTRID LINDGREN · INGRID NYMAN

Translated from Swedish by Margaret Turner

rabén&sjögren

It was a beautiful spring day, the sun was shining, the birds were twittering and snow water ran in all the ditches. Tommy and Annika came skipping over to Pippi's. Tommy had brought two lumps of sugar for the horse, and both he and Annika stopped for a moment in the porch to pat it before they went inside to see Pippi. Pippi was asleep when they came in. Her feet were on the pillow, and her head was far down under the bedclothes. She always slept that way. Annika pinched her big toe and called:

"Wake up!"

Mr Nilsson, the little monkey, was already awake and sitting on the lamp hanging from the ceiling. Presently there was movement underneath the bedclothes, and suddenly a red head popped out. Pippi opened her bright eyes, grinned, and said:

"Oh, it's you! I dreamt it was my father, looking to see if I had any corns."

She sat up, put her legs out and pulled on her stockings, one brown and the other black.

"Course not! You don't get any corns from these," she said, putting on her big, black shoes which were exactly twice as long as her feet.

"Pippi," said Tommy, "what shall we do? Annika and I have a holiday today."

"Ooh," said Pippi, "let's think up something nice. We can't dance round the Christmas tree, because we threw it out three months ago. Otherwise we could have played Christmas games all morning. It would be fun to dig for gold, but we can't do that either, because we don't know where the gold is. Besides, most of the gold is in Alaska, and you can't move an inch there for gold diggers. No, we must think of something else."

"Yes," said Annika, "something *really* nice."

Pippi did her hair into two tight plaits that stuck straight out. She was thinking.

"What about going into town to do some shopping?" she said at last.

"But we haven't got any money," said Tommy.

"I have," said Pippi, and to prove it she went at once and opened her suitcase which was full of gold coins. She took out a large handful and put the coins in a big pocket in the front of her apron.

"Now, if I could only find my hat," she said, "I'd be ready to start off."

The hat was nowhere to be seen. First Pippi took a look in the wood-box, but strange to say it was not there. Then she looked in the breadbin, but there was nothing in it except a suspender, a broken alarm clock, and a small rusk. Finally she looked on the hat rack, but found only a frying pan, a screw-driver, and a piece of cheese.

"There's no order in nothing, and I can't find everything," said Pippi irritably. "Though I've missed the cheese for a long time: good thing that was found. Come here, hat," she shouted, "are you coming shopping or not? If you don't come at once, you'll be too late!"

No hat came.

"Well, it has no one but itself to blame when it's so obstinate, but I won't put up with any complaints when I come back," she said sternly.

Soon afterwards they could be seen walking along the road leading to the centre of the town, Tommy and Annika and Pippi with Mr Nilsson on her shoulder. The sun shone brilliantly, the sky was very blue, and the children were very happy. There was a gurgling in the ditch beside the road. It was a deep ditch with lots of water in it.

"I like ditches," said Pippi, and without further ado she stepped down into the water. It went above her knees, and when she jumped really hard it splashed Tommy and Annika.

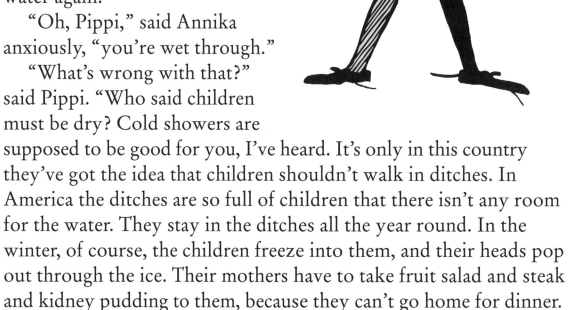

"I'm a boat," she said, and ploughed through the water. As she said this she stumbled and went under.

"I mean a submarine," she went on quite unperturbed as soon as her head was above water again.

"Oh, Pippi," said Annika anxiously, "you're wet through."

"What's wrong with that?" said Pippi. "Who said children must be dry? Cold showers are supposed to be good for you, I've heard. It's only in this country they've got the idea that children shouldn't walk in ditches. In America the ditches are so full of children that there isn't any room for the water. They stay in the ditches all the year round. In the winter, of course, the children freeze into them, and their heads pop out through the ice. Their mothers have to take fruit salad and steak and kidney pudding to them, because they can't go home for dinner. But, you bet, they're as strong and fit as can be."

The little town looked lovely in the spring sunshine. The narrow, cobbled streets seemed to wind their way anyhow between the rows of houses. Nearly every house was surrounded by a small garden with snowdrops and crocuses in it.

There were lots of shops in the little town. On this fine spring day plenty of people were going in and out of them, and the shop bells rang continuously. The housewives arrived with baskets on their arms to buy coffee and sugar and soap and butter. Quite a lot of children were out buying toffees or packets of chewing gum, but most of them had no money to spend, and these poor things stood outside the shops and could only *look* at all the sweets behind the glass.

When the sun was shining most brightly, three small people appeared in the High Street. They were Tommy, Annika, and Pippi — a very moist Pippi, who left a wet trail behind her as she sauntered along.

"Aren't we lucky?" said Annika. "Look at all the shops, and we have a pocketful of gold coins!"

Tommy was so happy when he thought of this that he jumped for joy.

"Shall we start then?" said Pippi. "First of all I'd like to buy a piano."

"But, Pippi," said Tommy, "you can't play the piano!"

"How should I know when I've never tried?" said Pippi. "I've never had a piano to practise on, and I tell you, Tommy, to play the piano without having a piano needs a lot of practice."

There was no piano shop in sight. Instead the children saw a perfumery shop. A large jar of freckle cream stood in the window, and beside the jar was an advertisement, saying: DO YOU SUFFER FROM FRECKLES?

"What does it say?" asked Pippi.

She could not read much, because she never wanted to go to school like other children.

"It says: 'DO YOU SUFFER FROM FRECKLES?'" said Annika.

"Oh, does it?" said Pippi thoughtfully. "Well, a polite question should have a polite answer. Come along, let's go in!"

She pushed the door open and walked in, closely followed by Tommy and Annika. An elderly lady was standing behind the counter. Pippi went straight up to her.

"No," she said firmly.

"What do you want, dear?" said the lady.

"No," said Pippi again.

"I don't know what you mean," said the lady.

"No, I do *not* suffer from freckles," said Pippi.

Then the lady understood, but, glancing at Pippi, she exclaimed:

"But, my dear child, your face is full of freckles!"

"Of course," said Pippi, "but I don't suffer from them. I like them! Good morning!"

She started to walk out, but in the doorway she turned round and called:

"But if you get any cream that makes *more* freckles, send me about seven or eight jars."

"We haven't done much shopping yet," said Pippi. "We really must get down to it."

Pippi marched on. She stopped at a sweet shop. A group of children was outside, gazing at all the wonderful things displayed in the window: large jars full of red and blue and green sweets, long rows of chocolate bars, piles and piles of chewing gum, and the most tempting toffee lollipops. No wonder the little children gazed and now and then heaved a heavy sigh, because they had no money, not even one little penny.

"Pippi, shall we go in?" said Tommy, eagerly tugging at Pippi's dress.

"We're *going* into this shop," said Pippi. "*Far* into it!"

And they entered.

"Please may I have thirty-six pounds of sweets," said Pippi, waving a gold coin in the air. The assistant only gaped. She was not used to anyone buying so many sweets at one time.

"You mean you want thirty-six sweets," she said.

"I mean that I want thirty-six *pounds* of sweets," said Pippi. She put the gold coin on the counter. The assistant hurriedly began pouring sweets into large bags. Tommy and Annika pointed to the sweets they thought the best. There were some red ones which were delicious; when you had sucked them for a while a lovely soft mixture oozed out. There were some green acid drops that were not bad either. The jelly babies and liquorice allsorts were jolly good, too.

"Let's have six pounds of each," suggested Annika. And they did.

"Then if you give me sixty lollipops and seventy-two small packets of toffee, I don't think I need to take more than one hundred and three chocolate cigarettes for today," said Pippi, "except perhaps a small cart to carry them in."

The assistant said she thought a cart could be bought at the toy shop close by.

By this time a lot of children had gathered outside the sweet shop. They were all staring through the window and gasped when they saw Pippi's way of doing her shopping. Pippi hurried into the toy shop, bought a cart, and loaded it with all the bags of sweets. She looked round and called out:

"Is there a child here who *does not* eat sweets? If so, will he or she please step forward."

No one stepped forward.

"Strange!" said Pippi. "Does there happen to be a child who *does* eat sweets, then?"

Twenty-three came forward, Tommy and Annika with them, of course.

"Tommy, open the bags!" said Pippi.

Tommy did so. A sweet-eating began, the like of which had never been seen in the little town. All the children filled their mouths with sweets, the red ones with the luscious juice inside, and the green acid ones, and the liquorice allsorts, and the jelly babies — all higgledy-piggledy. You could also have a chocolate cigarette in the corner of your mouth, because the taste of chocolate and jelly mixed was very nice. More children came running from every direction, and Pippi shared out handfuls all round.

"I think I shall have to buy another thirty-six pounds," she said, "otherwise there won't be anything for tomorrow."

Pippi bought another thirty-six pounds, but there was not much left for tomorrow in spite of it.

"Now we'll go to the next shop," said Pippi and stalked into the toy shop.

All the children followed. There were lots of nice things in the toy shop: trains and cars that could be wound up, pretty little dolls in beautiful dresses, dolls' china, and toy pistols, and tin soldiers, and soft toy dogs and elephants, and bookmarks, and jumping-jacks …

"Can I help you?" said the assistant.

"I'd like some of everything," said Pippi, examining the shelves. "We need, for instance, jumping-jacks and toy pistols," she continued, "but that can easily be put right, I expect."

As she spoke Pippi pulled out a whole handful of gold coins, and then the children had to point out what they thought they needed most. Annika decided on a doll with fair, curly hair and a pink silk dress which could say 'mama' when you pressed its tummy. Tommy wanted a toy gun and a steam engine — and got them.

All the other children pointed at what they wanted, and when Pippi had finished buying there was not much left in the shop, except for a few bookmarks and some building blocks. Pippi did not buy a single thing for herself, but Mr Nilsson got a mirror.

Just before they left, Pippi bought each child a toy ocarina, and when they were all out in the street again they played their ocarinas. One little boy complained that his instrument would not work. Pippi took a look at it.

"No wonder, when there's chewing gum in it! Where did you pick up this treasure?" she asked, throwing away the large white ball. "I don't remember buying any chewing gum."

"I've had it since last Friday," said the boy.

"Aren't you afraid your lips will grow together? That's what I thought usually happened to chewing gum chewers."

She gave the boy back his ocarina, and he blew it merrily with the rest. There was such a noise in the High Street that at last a policeman came to see what was going on.

"What's all this?" he shouted.

"It's the Regimental March of the Grenadiers," said Pippi, "but I'm not sure all the children realize it. Some of them seem to think we're playing 'Out roared the Dreadful Thunder'."

"Stop it!" yelled the policeman, covering his ears with his hands. Pippi patted him soothingly on the back.

"You can thank your lucky stars we didn't buy trumpets," she said.

One by one the ocarinas stopped playing. Finally it was only Tommy's that gave a little squeak now and then. The policeman told them sternly that crowds were not allowed to collect in the High Street, and that the children must go home at once. The children did not mind. They were anxious to try out their toy trains and drive their motor-cars and make up the beds for their new dolls, so they all went home, happy and contented. They could not be bothered with supper that day.

It was time for Pippi and Tommy and Annika to go home, too. Pippi pulled the truck. She noticed all the shop signs as she passed them, and tried to spell as well as she could.

# APOTHECARY

"*Apu-the-ca-ry*. Goodness! Isn't that where you buy meducin?" she asked.

"Yes, that's where you buy *medicine*," said Annika.

"Ooh, then I must go in straight away and buy some," said Pippi.

"But you're not ill," said Tommy.

"I may not be ill now," said Pippi, "but I'm not taking any chances. Every year masses of people are taken ill and die, all because they didn't buy meducin in time: you bet I'm not going to be caught out that way."

The apothecary was rolling pills, but he intended to roll only a few more because it was late, and near closing time. Then Pippi and Tommy and Annika walked up to the counter.

"Please can I have six pints of meducin?" said Pippi.

"What kind?" asked the apothecary impatiently.

"Well," said Pippi, "one that's good for illness."

"What kind of illness?" asked the apothecary, still more impatiently.

"I think I'd like one that's good for whooping cough and blisters on the feet and tummy-ache and German measles and a pea that's got stuck in the nose, and all that kind of thing. It wouldn't be a bad idea if it could be used for polishing furniture as well. A real meducin, that's what I want."

The apothecary said that no medicine was quite like that. There were different kinds of medicine for different illnesses, he explained, and when Pippi had mentioned about ten other complaints which she also wanted cured, he put a row of bottles on the counter.

On some of them he wrote, "For external use only," which meant that the medicine was only meant to be applied to the skin. Pippi paid, took her bottles, thanked him and walked out.

Tommy and Annika followed her. The apothecary looked at the clock and saw that it was time to close the shop. He locked the door carefully after the children and thought how nice it would be to go home to a meal.

Pippi put her bottles down on the doorstep.

"Oh, dear me," she said. "I nearly forgot the most important thing."

As the door was now shut, she put her finger on the bell and rang long and hard. Tommy and Annika heard the shrill sound inside the shop. Presently a small window in the door was opened; this was the window through which you could buy medicine for people who fell ill at night. The apothecary popped his head out. His face was rather red.

"What do you want now?" he asked Pippi in a gruff voice.

"Please, Mr Aputhecary," said Pippi, "I've just thought of something. You know all about illness: what's really best for a tummy-ache? To eat black pudding or to put the whole tummy to soak in cold water?"

The apothecary's face became redder still.

"Be off with you, this very instant," he shouted, "or else … !"

He shut the window with a bang.

"Goodness, he's bad-tempered," said Pippi. "You'd almost think I'd annoyed him."

She rang the bell again, and it was not many seconds before the apothecary's head appeared once more in the window. His face was as red as a beetroot.

"Black pudding is perhaps a little indigestible?" suggested Pippi, looking up at him with friendly eyes. The apothecary made no reply, but simply slammed the window shut.

"Very well, then," said Pippi, shrugging her shoulders, "I'll just have to try black pudding, that's all. He'll only have himself to blame if it does me harm."

She calmly sat down on the steps outside the shop and arranged all her bottles in a row.

"My goodness, how unpractical grown-ups can be!" she said. "There are — let's see — eight bottles, and one bottle would easily hold the lot. Lucky I've got some commonsense myself," and she uncorked the bottles and emptied all the medicine into one of them. She shook it vigorously, and raising it to her mouth, she drank a large dose. Annika, knowing that some of the medicine was meant for putting on the skin, was rather worried.

"Oh, Pippi," she said, "how do you know that the medicine isn't poisonous?"

"I shall find out," said Pippi gaily. "I shall find out tomorrow at the latest. If I'm still alive then, it's not poisonous, and the smallest child can drink it."

Tommy and Annika considered this. After a while Tommy said doubtfully, and rather dolefully:

"Yes, but supposing it is poisonous, after all, what then?"

"Then you'll have to use what's left over for polishing the dining-room furniture," said Pippi, "and poisonous or not, the meducin won't be wasted."

She took the bottle and placed it on the cart. It already contained Tommy's steam engine and toy gun, and Annika's doll, and a bag with five small sweets which was all that was left of the two thirty-six pounds. Mr Nilsson was sitting in it, too. He was tired, and wanted to go home.

"Besides, I can tell you, I think it's a jolly good meducin. I feel better already. I feel terrifically well, and fit for anything," said Pippi, marching along jauntily.

Off she went, with the cart, back to Villekulla Cottage. Tommy and Annika walked beside her feeling just a little queer in the tummy.